ROY PENDLE

The Old Jack Tales

Illustrated by Bridget Bravo

For my girls, with love.

Old Jack is a conundrum... part legend and part fable that's woven deep into Tiritane folklore.

Old Jack represents someone or something, be it human, animal, or even a feeling. Old Jack can be a villain or a hero, or maybe just a way of explaining the unknown.

Solar System 451 of the Federal Galaxy Administration, Tiritane sits on the very edge of the Milky Way, almost in the void. The Old Jack Tales is a collection of fifteen sci-fi folk stories set in the far future many millennia from now.

CONTENTS

DANNY LOSES HIS WAY

Danny couldn't find the path. He'd been wandering around for an hour now and the evening twilight had faded into darkness. The argument with Elaine had been serious and there was no coming back from an announcement like that. He hadn't been thinking about where he was walking and it had started to rain. The trees had been dense enough to hold off some of the downpour so he'd taken cover under a large pine for a few minutes before heading off in completely the wrong direction.

His coat was in the shuttle of course and the temperature was dropping quickly. Winter on Hilos 381 is usually mild but night time temperatures could be as low as one or two degrees, certainly cold enough to get hypothermia if you go out and about in a thin tunic. Danny had his personal communicator with him but there was some kind of atmospheric interference going on and the directional phase emitter linked to the shuttle was just spinning randomly.

With a low moon and only faint starlight between wispy

clouds to see by, Danny started to worry. He couldn't shout for help, not after the surgery on his neck from the pulse burn incident, he could only talk in a hoarse whisper. Shouting probably wouldn't help anyway and would possibly bring more trouble. Danny didn't know what kind of animals inhabited the forest but, going on some of the noises he was hearing, he thought it best to keep a low profile and keep moving.

Another hour passed by and he was still no nearer to finding his shuttle, though at least his antique chronodial was still working. He was glad he had upgraded to the ten year battery but he wasn't sure how long ago he traded the first gen pistol pulse for it, three or four years perhaps. Just as the shivering started to make his teeth chatter he glimpsed a light flickering off in the distance.

His initial reaction was to run towards the light but his training told him to take it carefully and close in without making any noise. He crept in and around the dense bushes as softly as he could, finally coming to an open glade where he could see the silhouette of a large man stacking logs next to a fire. Danny leaned forward and was about to take a step out into the glade when a hand covered his mouth and he was jerked back.

The initial shock and indignation that someone had taken him by surprise was made far worse by the fact that his captor was female. It wasn't so much that she had been strong enough to take him out silently, it was because he hadn't seen a woman for nearly a year, not since setting off on his latest mission.

The tall female dressed in fur lined animal skins, put a finger up to her lips to emphasise he should stay silent before whispering in a low voice, 'That's Old Jack the wood cutter. He's got a very sharp axe and he hates strangers trespassing in his woods. He will kill anyone he finds, especially Tiritane fly boys like you.'

Danny put his hands up in surrender and they moved silently back from the glade. After fifty metres or so, Danny whispered a thank you to his new friend as they quietly hunkered down behind a large thicket. The woman pulled a blanket from her backpack and put it around Danny's shoulders.

'I'm Danny, a band two Pilot-Officer, of the Tiritane Exploration Service.'

'Greetings Danny, I am Kiren. What are you doing in the forest at night without proper clothing?' she asked with a disparaging look.

'Ah yes, I err, left my shuttle for a walk and got lost. My communicator isn't working and I feel like a bit of an idiot now.' said Danny embarrassingly. 'Have you seen it? Can you help me find it?'

'Yes, it is two hundred and fifty metres that way.' replied Kiren, pointing west. 'You really shouldn't go wandering about these woods you know; you fly boys are stupid, you're the second one this year.'

'I knew it! I told Elaine that Simon's shuttle had come to this planet but it didn't believe me. It threatened to report me to the service for being out of my sector. For an Artificial Intelligence it can be really stupid at times.'

'Well I suggest you get back to the shuttle and go to your sector like Elaine says. It's very dangerous here Danny.'

'No, I need to find Simon. It's his first proper mission. He's only seventeen and he's my little brother.'

'Your brother is dead Danny, I saw Old Jack kill him.'

Danny gasped in shock, he couldn't believe it. He had been searching for his brother for the last three months, even flying out of his sector. Now he'd finally tracked him down, only to discover he'd been murdered by an axe wielding psychopath.

'But are you definitely sure it was Simon that Old Jack killed?' he asked with a look of horror in his eyes.

'Oh yes, his name was on his tunic, just like yours.'

Danny was in shock, barely believing what he was hearing. Overcome by grief and then a sudden rage, he stood up clenching his fists.

'Right, I'm going to kill Old Jack. He's going to suffer like Simon did.'

'No Danny, you must go. Old Jack is far too strong and vicious. You could never beat him.'

'I could with your help Kiren, you're very strong. I'm sure we could take him together.'

'Well, I know he can be very mean at times, but I could never do that. I love my husband far too much to kill him.'

ERICA'S CHALLENGE

Erica unzipped the tent flap and crawled out onto the frosty grass. It had been very cold in the night, well below freezing. It was just before dawn and the first rays of the sun were reflecting off the wispy cloud making it look a pinkish red. Erica was warm enough though so her thick thermal sleeping bag had done its job.

It was Erica's birthday, she didn't feel much different than she had the day before but she knew today was going to be the biggest challenge of her life. It was a ritual, a rite of passage, which every young person in her village went through on day they turned thirteen.

Yesterday, she had walked the fifteen miles on her own with her pack weighing heavy on her back. Erica had climbed up the steep track up to the top of Eagle Ridge to set-up camp and take in the estuary below. It was vast with a small island about a thousand metres from the shore.

It didn't have a name, it was just known as the island. Every teenager in her village had been there. Some had never returned, some had returned empty handed. If you returned without the prize you were cast out, never to be welcomed home. That was the price to pay for failure.

Erica didn't know if the teenagers who hadn't returned had got lost, been killed, or just couldn't face the shame and rejection. Maybe they had decided to go and make a life elsewhere. She had seen the hurt and pain of the parents whose children had not come back and sometimes they left too, to find them, or take their shame from the village.

'I will not fail.' said Erica out loud to the wind. There was no one to hear her, or so she thought... She did not think about whether the challenge was right or wrong, to send a young person out on such a dangerous quest. All she cared about was going back to her parents in triumph and being the pride of the village.

Erica stowed her gear into her pack and left it on the well-worn stone shelf. She was going to swim to the island in the freezing water with her knife on her leather belt and her hunting spear in its sling over her shoulder. She was not as tall as some of her friends but she was the fastest sprinter, and that would matter she told herself, as she tied up her shoulder length black hair into a pony tail and put her soft leather running shoes on.

The hunters in the village used speeders and pulse lasers these days but this was old school, it had to be done traditionally to honour the village.

The tide was on the turn, just going out, and the water was very cold but she had done her training every day swimming in the river as instructed by her father and she could tolerate it well. She swam at a steady pace knowing she would need all her energy later on the island

As Erica stood up and took her first step onto the island a blow to the top of her head knocked her off her feet and she landed face down with a mouthful of sand. She pulled herself up quickly and ran towards the trees. Blood was running down her face and mixing with the sand in the corner of her mouth. She threw herself into a large bush that was full of thorns biting into her. She would be safe there she thought, at least for now.

The sea eagle had come swooping down from behind as she finished her swim. She hadn't seen or heard it but she knew it was Old Jack, the massive sea eagle that protected the island. Erica knew she had to outwit Old Jack somehow to get the prize, claim her place in the village and win the love of her people.

Spitting out the sand and blood, Erica stemmed the flow from her head with a cloth from her small bag. The cut wasn't too deep, and luckily she had stumbled slightly as she stood up from the water's edge. Otherwise she would have been seriously injured or dead from the huge talon that had glanced through her hairline.

Erica was an only child and she knew her parents would be worried about her, especially her mother. She had barely made it back herself and had never spoken about her challenge at all. Her father was much more positive, always telling Erica she would succeed, always boosting her confidence, even when she made mistakes in her training. She needed those memories now, she had to get herself together and beat Old Jack.

The prize was a nut, the seed of a great tree that sat in the clearing at the centre of the island. It was an ancient tree and the only one of its kind left. It fruited every year but the seeds never germinated. Teardrop in shape, they were about four centimetres long and one centimetre thick in the middle, a bit like a large apple pip. When you triumphantly brought it home, it was made into a pendant to wear around your neck.

It was part of your identity, the village's identity.

'You will fail,' came the words, dark and threatening, as a large shadow engulfed the bush Erica was crouching in. Old Jack had settled down onto the branch of the large pine above her. Without hesitation, Erica launched her spear upwards towards the massive bird. It came close but Old Jack twisted his great body to one side watching it flash by.

'We shall see,' said Erica leaping out of the bush running towards the middle of the island hoping the trees would give her enough cover. Old Jack sprung up into the air and tracked her progress to the edge of the clearing settling onto another branch, poised to strike as soon as she would leave the tree line.

With her spear lost, Erica only had her knife left to defend herself. It had been a present from her father on her sixth birthday. The knife was her most treasured possession. It had a carved bone handle worn smooth and a razor sharp blade with a slight curve. About thirty centimetres in total length, the knife had been handed down through the generations and she was immensely proud to bear it.

Erica could see some seeds lying on the ground under the great tree. The winter had come and the fruit had rotted away. She knew Old Jack would be on her as soon as she left the cover of the pinewood, but somehow she had to acquire a prize to take home.

Taking a deep breath, Erica sprinted out into the clearing counting every step just like she rehearsed with her father many times. Old Jack launched from his perch swooping down fast with his lethal talons reaching out towards her.

Eleven, twelve, thirteen, this was it – Erica launched into a forward roll as Old Jack's talons sliced through the air millimetres above her stooping head. She completed the roll and came to her feet again launching the knife with all her might as he sped past her. Trying to twist around and sweep back for another pass, the knife tore through Old Jack's right wing, taking out some feathers and nicking into the bone.

Old Jack tumbled over and over before crashing into the base of the great tree in a heap. Erica ran forward again picking up a seed. Turning to run back to the treeline she suddenly froze. Was Old Jack dead? Mortally wounded? Just dazed? She had to know.

A sudden thought struck her: if he was dead the challenge would be over forever, teenagers would easily be able to get the prize from now on. The danger would be gone and everyone would safely return home to their families. Erica would be a hero having vanquished the mighty enemy. She had to find out.

Erica approached Old Jack slowly and carefully. He was still alive but he was badly injured. She retrieved her precious knife and raised it ready to give the final strike but then she hesitated, and instead, pulled the cloth from her small bag and bound the injury on Old Jack's wing. She gently sat him up and went off to hunt some rabbit, finding her spear on the way.

As she laid two rabbits at his feet, Old Jack opened his eyes and looked at her half dazed.

'Why would you do such a thing? I would have given you no quarter.'

'Because our village needs you Old Jack. If you were not here, how could we prove ourselves? How could we become adults and show our worth as hunters?'

'You have shown me a great kindness when you could have run away and left me to die. I thank you. Tell me your name child, it can be the tell word for your offspring. I will allow them a free pass as a reward for your actions today.'

'My name is Erica, but none shall utter it, my children will earn their prize as we all have.'

Erica bowed to Old Jack and turned to make her journey home. She would not tell anyone how she had won her prize. It was not the way of the villagers to brag.

RIN AND THE TOWER

Rin took off into the sky, his heart racing and his wings spreading as far as they could go. The wind off the sea today was fierce, blowing a gale through the trees that were bent over at angle. The trees acted like a wedge causing a great up draft. Rin and all the other young crows loved days like this, hovering, swooping, and soaring for hours on end.

Rin's father Rosen hovered beside him for a moment or two before nodding over towards the tower.

'Follow me Rin, we need to talk.'

That sounded ominous to Rin, what could be so important that a private talk was required? That hardly ever happened.

Alighting softly onto the sill of the only first floor window, Rosen began to speak in a low tone barely loud enough for Rin to hear.

'Your great grandfather needs your help son. You must fly to the top of the tower at nightfall, no one must see you and you must not tell anyone. It must be a secret meeting.'

'But why father, what does great grandfather want me to

help him with?'

'I do not know Rin, but when you are summoned by Old Jack the keeper of the tower, you do not question. Just do your duty as a King's Crow even if you are only a Junior Guardian.'

Rin had never met his great grandfather. Old Jack was a legend who was occasionally seen on the crenulations at the top of the ten storey round tower. He was old, very old, everyone either revered him or was scared of him. Rin both revered and feared him due to his mighty reputation.

As a Junior Guardian, his duties so far had been to watch the coast for human ships. It was by far the easiest and most enjoyable task with the prevailing wind letting him hover and soar. Adult crows patrolled inland, sweeping over the long peninsula right up to the stone land bridge five miles away.

Rin had never seen a ship, or a human for that matter. Well not a real one. His father hadn't either but Rin's grandfather Jaren had. Jaren was Keeper of the Key for the first floor and once a year the door was unlocked for all the King's Crows to enter and see the painted frescoes on the walls showing images of people and ships.

Every evening as the darkness drew in all the crows except a few bridge guardians gathered at the base of the great tower for the Tell. The Tell was a report from all areas of the peninsula and out to the bridge. The harsh and raucous cawing sounds travelled all the way up to the very top of the tower where Old Jack listened intently.

That evening, Rin stood next to his great grandfather and heard the Tell from the top of the tower. He was nervous, not knowing why he was there.

'Rin, do you have a mate yet?'

This took Rin by surprise, no one had asked him that before but he had recently taken up with Lorel and the bond was strong.

'Yes, Keeper of the Tower,' replied Rin.

'Good, when your first son hatches in the spring, you will come to me and take my place. I will teach you the answers to the three questions that any human who claims kingship will have to know before this key is given over.'

Old Jack held up a key in his beak, the key to the chest on the top floor of the tower that contained the crown. The crown that had been guarded safely for two hundred years. Rin was so shocked, he had no idea this was to be his fate, to become the Keeper of the Tower awaiting the return of the King.

The winter came and went and when the spring arrived, Rin named his first son Jack. He waited until nightfall and nervously flew to the top of the tower like he had before. He and Old Jack listened to the Tell and then Old Jack settled to roost.

'In the morning Rin, I will teach you the questions and answers. I will announce you as my successor, then I will fly to the sea and be no more.'

First light came and Rin looked out, there was a gale picking up and he was a little sad to think he would no longer be able to float or soar on the wind. He had his duty to do and keep up the honour of the King's Crows, guardians of the Crown. Today he will become Keeper of the Tower and learn the King's secrets.

Just then a mighty call came up on the wind, all the young crows were calling. There was a ship on the horizon, a huge hover ship with two large ion engines at the back and a large gold banner flying proudly from the prow. The banner had a black crown above a crow emblazoned on it.

'Great grandfather, the King returns to claim his crown!'

shouted Rin excitedly. But when he turned around, Old Jack was on his roost, still as stone. Then the key dropped to the floor with a clatter, Old Jack was dead!

ARVAN TO THE RESCUE

Arvan was trying to think as quickly as he could.

'Arvan if you do not eject in the next forty seconds you will be killed when the Bluesonic core explodes.'

'But Kal, I'll drown in the ocean if I eject now! We're too far from the island. There must be something else I can do?'

Arvan was trying desperately not to panic but he was running out of options. He had already regretted his decision to follow the distress beacon co-ordinates, even though it was his job. As a band three Tiritane Explorer, he was duty bound to offer help in any way he could.

'Kal, what if we blow the emergency release bolts on the engine housing and separate the hull from the cockpit? We could glide the cockpit section towards the island and then the seawater will cool the Bluesonic core. We might even find a way to reattach it later.'

'Ok, that might work. You will have to glide manually and the instant loss of power will render me inactive, you will be on your own Arvan.'

'Do it, do it now!'

'Primed and set for three, two, bye Arvan.'

The bolts blew all at once and the hull started to fall away. The cockpit nose suddenly sprang upwards and Arvan had to fight with the controls to level off. Kal could be really annoying and was often sarcastic but Arvan was missing his AI already.

The hull hit the water a few seconds later with a huge splashdown. Arvan was still fighting with the steering column, waiting for the massive explosion of the Bluesonic core. The cockpit skimmed the water three times before the nose violently entered the ocean at an acute angle. Two minutes later, Arvan woke up with water pouring into the cockpit and onto his face from a crack in the polyglass shield.

The cockpit was the right way up but it was damaged beyond repair and the only way out was for Arvan to eject. He pulled the handle and twisted it left then right. He was catapulted upwards and as he hit the water again he released his harness and started swimming towards the island, still 300 metres away.

Looking around, there was no large plume of smoke so Arvan assumed the Bluesonic core had not blown up. That was something he thought but it was still pretty much a disaster. Just as he was mulling this over he glimpsed some shapes moving in the water, some type of fin. It took a few seconds before it sank in – oh crap, sharks!

His helmet was still attached to his suit by the coms cord and he grabbed it just in time to swing down hard on the nose of the first shark. Three more were circling around and just as they came at him, a huge wave came over from behind and he was launched out of the water momentarily. He was badly winded from the impact but when he checked, all his limbs were miraculously still attached.

A very large dolphin had come in at pace and the sharks disappeared immediately. The dolphin came back around and one of its flippers came into the crook of Arvan's armpit and he was propelled forwards toward the island. Arvan could see the island clearly now, it was a huge volcanic emergence looming out of the ocean. The sides were steep and there was no beach or landing point, just enormous cliffs. There appeared to be no way to get onto the island.

Just as Arvan thought they were going to crash into the cliff wall, the dolphin dived down taking Arvan with it. He held his breath for what seemed like an eternity and just as he started to pass out he could feel hands around him pulling him onto a rocky shore.

'Welcome traveller,' came a deep voice, 'are you ok, are you injured?'

Arvan got to his feet with a little help, he was sopping wet and a bit confused but he wasn't injured. There were fifty to sixty people standing on the rocky shore, looking at him with amazement. He could only string a few words together.

'Sharks – dolphin – shuttle broken.'

'Oh yes, Old Jack the dolphin, he saved you from the sharks. He has been helping us for many years.' came the deep voice again.

'When the seas rose and we were trapped here forty years ago, he came and brought us fish to eat. We have fresh water from the spring, roots grow and we have leaves too, but we would have starved without Old Jack.'

Just as Arvan opened his mouth to speak, Old Jack emerged from the sea hole behind him, launching the Bluesonic core in its titanium suspension rack onto the rocks.

'He wants you to take that to the temple,' said the old man with the deep voice.

Arvan was stunned, 'Wait, what, you can understand him?

That's incredible.'

'Oh yes, I have sat on this rock on and off for thirty years, we have an understanding.'

Arvan picked up the core and followed the man to the middle of the volcano. Right there in the centre was a building but it wasn't a temple, it was a space shuttle. It was very ergonomically shaped with fantastic curls and swept back wings. On the front below the polyglass bubble was the registration, 01D-J4CK.

The cockpit section was full of a strange glowing fluid and for a moment Arvan didn't understand. Then suddenly it came to him, Old Jack the dolphin was the pilot. Arvan nearly fell over with shock and the old man had to steady him.

'The atmosphere broke his engine like it did to your ship. He came to answer our call when the world overheated and the glaciers melted. He says if you connect your power cell to his temple, his people will get a signal and rescue us all.'

ROMESH MUST WIN

Romesh was fed up. He never won, never getting the largest best mushroom from the forest floor. Jas, his big sister, one of the twins, always got there first. She had the best speeder and it gave her the advantage. It was a family tradition to race into the woods every year to find and bring back the best fungi for father to roast on the wood fire grill.

Anika had the same model of speeder as Jas but she didn't maintain it as well, and that gave Jas the advantage. Romesh was determined to win this year whatever it took. Being the youngest was so frustrating, you couldn't do anything or go anywhere on your own. It had been great while Davin was still at home. As brothers they spent lots of time together, sharing a room and going on adventures.

Davin left to join the Tiritane Exploration Service three years ago when he turned fifteen. Romesh missed him terribly and the incessant teasing from his twelve year old sisters was becoming unbearable. For a nine year old, Romesh was fairly handy with a set of spanners and he had a plan. He had been secretly restoring Davin's old speeder and that was going to give him the edge he needed.

Davin's speeder was bigger and more powerful than Romesh's. It was an adult model and Romesh could just about reach the handlebar. All the dust and grime was cleaned off and it gleamed ready for action. This time, said Romesh to himself, no annoying girl is going to beat me.

'Romesh hurry up or the girls will start without you.' came his father's voice.

Jas and Anika were lined up side by side, ready for the three kilometre race to the woods. They were throttling their speeders waiting impatiently for the race to start. Romesh rode Davin's speeder out of the workshop and came up beside them.

Everyone was startled by the sight of Romesh barely balancing on the great machine, and before his father could say no, Romesh hit the throttle booster button and took off like a rocket. His sisters tore off after him but he was already three hundred metres in front and stretching out a big lead.

It took no time before the forest came into view, it was wide but shallow, and maybe a hundred and fifty metres deep. Just beyond the forest was the cliff edge, a sheer drop of four hundred metres to the sea.

Romesh remembered the fireside stories his father used to tell about a terrible monster who lived on a narrow ledge on the cliff face, just below the edge. Old Jack the cliff ghast was huge with sharp teeth, long arms and razor sharp claws. He would spring up and catch unsuspecting birds as they flew out of the woods or leap onto the cliff top and drag small animals or naughty children down to his ledge and eat them. Ha, just stories to scare young boys and girls enough to stay in their beds and not go wandering off thought Romesh.

The trees were coming up fast now and Romesh realised he would have to slow down, he was far enough in front to have a big advantage in finding the largest mushroom and he knew the best spot to find it.

Romesh twisted the throttle back and hit the reverse thruster button. To his horror, nothing happened. He hit the button again and again to no avail. He was at the tree line now and he desperately swerved left and right trying to avoid the great pines. The back end of the speeder clipped a tree and the sudden jerk threw Romesh off before the speeder crashed head on into a large pine.

Romesh tumbled over and over. How he missed the last tree was a miracle as he rolled out onto the cliff top coming to a stop about ten metres before the edge. His knees and elbows were all grazed and red. There was blood trickling down from his nose and his head was spinning. Still dizzy from the tumbling, Romesh tried to stand up but his right leg wouldn't support him and he fell down again.

That's when he heard it – the blood curdling shriek from below the cliff edge – Romesh started to panic and crawl his way back to the trees but it was too late. A great beast with wild eyes and long sharp teeth bounded over towards him in a mighty leap. Romesh closed his eyes and waited for the inevitable snap of those fierce jaws to engulf him.

Just then, the sound of a speeder emerging out of the woods and screeching into a broadside made Romesh open his eyes and look up. Jas was flying through the air feet first, slamming into the beast's chest and knocking it onto its back. It was up again in a flash just as a second speeder burst through the trees. Anika swung a large branch violently around her head, hitting the ghast in the face and making it stumble backwards. Jas ran forwards and grabbed its arm swinging it over the cliff. It screamed all the way to the bottom then came silence.

Jas and Anika picked Romesh up and put him on the back of Jas's speeder and they started for home.

'You boys really are stupid, it's no wonder you never get past band three of the service,' said Jas, looking over her shoulder to make sure Romesh was still holding on. 'One day I'm going to be in band five, the fighter squadron, like mum, just you wait and see.'

Romesh hugged his sister tightly, she was his new hero.

'Thank you Jas, for saving me from Old Jack, he would have eaten me alive if it wasn't for you.'

'Oh no, that's wasn't Old Jack, that was one of his little boys; he is way bigger and stronger, you just remember that Romesh.

JANE MEETS THE MAYOR

Jane was new to the little town of Storm Haven, having only moved in the day before. It was late in the afternoon as she walked along the jetty looking at the power-jet boats returning from the sea with their catches of fish. It was a pretty little fishing town, well hardly a town, more like a big village with lots of old cottages and a few tea shops.

She was thinking about what to have for supper when a very large one-legged seagull, swooped down and pecked at her with its bill. This happened three or four times and in the end she had to run in to the Crab Pot tea shop to escape. Jane was shaken by the experience but the owner of the tea shop, Sandra, smiled and sat her down with a cup of tea.

'So, you've met Old Jack the seagull. He's a nasty piece of work isn't he?'

'Yeah, what's all that about? He gave me a real fright, I thought I might lose an eye or something.'

'Well,' said Sandra, 'you didn't show him the respect he wanted.' as she buttered a toasted tea cake and brought it to

Jane.

'Respect, what do you mean? That sounds daft.'

'Old Jack was once the Town Mayor, he was a war hero who lost his leg in the battle of Krygos. It got sliced off by a laser cannon. He was a popular mayor, but over time, the adulation and power went to his head. He became greedy, building a large wealth from taxing the townsfolk.'

Jane burst out laughing. 'No, you're having me on, that sounds ridiculous.'

'It's all true I tell you. The old woman Marnah, who lived in the end cottage, the one you've just moved into. She refused to pay and when Jack tried to have her arrested she cast a spell on him. She stole his titanium leg and turned him into a seagull. Did you notice the gold crest around his neck?'

Jane couldn't stop laughing and Sandra became somewhat indignant.

'You'll see,' said Sandra, 'mark my words, if you say 'Good Morning, or Good Evening mister Mayor.' he won't attack you.'

Jane finished her toasted tea cake and drained her cup. She put her coat back on for the short walk to her cottage at the end of the lane. Old Jack was balancing on the jetty rail, looking particularly mean. Now that she looked properly she could see the gold coloured crest marking on his neck. Although she felt really stupid, she didn't dare risk another attack. So she nodded and said 'Good evening Mr Mayor.' Old Jack turned his head away and flew off. Jane went home chuckling to herself. Her ex-husband had told her she was a nut case for giving up her highly paid job in the city to go and live in a smelly old fishing town. She couldn't help thinking he might be right.

The next day when Jane visited the Crab Pot again, she and Sandra watched a number of people being terrorised by Old Jack. It looked amusing to start with, people were running all over the place trying to dodge him but as Sandra said, it wasn't good for the town. It was driving people away and businesses were suffering.

'Has anyone tried to get rid of him, you know like take him out with a pulse laser or something?'

'No, they are a protected species these days,' replied Sandra disconsolately.

'Do you think he will ever just go away then?'

'If the story is true, he won't leave while his false leg is still in the village and nobody knows where it's hidden.'

A couple of weeks went by and the builders finally started on the renovations Jane wanted. While they were taking down the badly cracked ceiling boards to replace them with new ones, Old Jack's titanium leg fell out of the rafters. Jane was gobsmacked and ran down to the Crab Pot immediately to tell Sandra, nodding a 'Good morning Mr Mayor,' as she went.

They settled down with a nice cuppa and hatched their plan. Jane would bring the leg to Sandra at midnight when Old Jack would be asleep. Sandra would give it to Davey the fisherman and he would stow it on his power-jet boat before setting out at dawn. He would take it far out to sea and throw it overboard.

Jane was really nervous as she sneaked her way down the lane to the back door of the Crab Pot with the false leg hidden under her long coat. It was a dark night and there was no sign of Old Jack. If her ex could see her now he would be falling about laughing thought Jane. Sandra took the titanium limb across to Davey's boat before returning to make tea and toast whilst waiting for the dawn to come. The next morning Davey's power-jet boat left the little harbour at top speed with

Old Jack flying hard behind it, never to be seen again.

SAM'S INHERITANCE

Sam tripped over a root sticking up across the path. He had been running as fast as he could after the roar of the bear had startled him into a panic. Pulling himself up again, the pain in his knee made him limp but he could still move quite quickly.

He climbed onto his speeder and headed for the town. The folk there had warned him about Old Jack the grizzly bear but it hadn't put him off. His father had told him long ago that an alien craft had crash landed into the mountain and that the site was guarded by a great bear. His father had seen the craft himself and watched as the alien creature emerged badly wounded and died.

Richard had a reputation for telling tall tales and often exaggerated events, especially when he had had a few beers, so the locals were very sceptical about his story of the alien craft. Sam first heard the story when he was young, maybe five or six. He was all grown up now, well he'd decided fifteen was grown up even though his mother didn't seem to think so. She had left Richard when Sam was ten, she couldn't take any more ridiculous drunken tales.

Richard died a year ago and Sam missed his father very much. He had only seen him a couple of times in the last three years and his loss was hard on him. Then came the parcel in the post from his father's lawyer: a small wooden box that contained a piece of metal, the metal was black with silver shapes inscribed on it.

The shapes appeared to be random squiggles. It was thin, two and a half centimetres wide, a centimetre thick and twenty centimetres long. There was a note in the box in his father's handwriting and it just said, 'return to alien craft but respect the bear.' Sam was beside himself with excitement and was determined to fulfil his father's last wish. He felt a bit stupid now for running away on his speeder but by the time he got back to town he had resolved to try again the following day.

The next morning Sam trekked up the mountain, watching carefully for any sign of the bear. He had lain awake most of the night thinking about his father's note. How could he respect the bear? How was he supposed to make Old Jack understand that he just wanted to return the strange metal bar?

Turning off the track and heading towards the dark looking cave set back into the bushes, Sam had a really nervous feeling. His still wasn't sure what to do about Old Jack but he had to go through with it. He stopped for a moment to take a swig of water then said to himself right it's now or never and he marched forthrightly towards the entrance. Old Jack came bounding out towards him, roaring like he had the day before.

Instead of running away this time, Sam knelt down on one knee, bowed his head and held up the bar. He closed his eyes and waited. A few seconds later he nervously opened them again, but Old Jack was nowhere to be seen.

The cave entrance was now lit up and Sam realised it was the entrance to a ship, a star ship. As Sam stepped into the ship he turned around and saw Old Jack sat in front of the door quietly waiting and suddenly realised it wasn't a bear at all. Old Jack the grizzly bear was a hologram! He could barely believe it, what a great defence it had been.

The star ship was small and it looked designed for just one being. Sam sat down in the seat in front of the screen with maps showing star constellations, then he remembered the metal bar. There was a vertical slot in the console and when Sam offered it up, it fitted seamlessly. All of a sudden the console started to flash. A series of shapes appeared one at a time on the screen, each one replaced by another. Sam had a sinking feeling in the pit of his stomach and then it dawned on him - oh crap, it's a countdown!

Sam tried to get out of the seat but large harness straps automatically rolled over his shoulders and clamped him in tight. There was a loud vibration and other strange noises before the door closed and the mountain started to shake.

JADE'S REVENGE

Jade was a quiet girl and a bit timid, making her mother worry about her all the time. Her younger brothers were boisterous to say the least but at fourteen years old she was practically a recluse, hardly ever coming out of her room.

Most girls Jade's age were in clubs or academies in preparation to join one of the exploration services. Her mother had been a band two pilot of a power-jet boat, escorting the huge ion hover ships in and out of port. When Jade's father died four years ago she'd had to put her career on hold to look after the children.

Jade had been very close to her father and they often went fishing at night to the great lake a kilometre from the town. The lake was very big, four kilometres long by one and a half wide. For three years from the age of seven, Jade and Jacob spent many happy nights under the great nebula fishing and chatting all about animals and nature.

The townsfolk relied on the lake for fish, the staple diet for the poor community of a rural backwater. The city was an expensive place to live and only people who worked for one of the exploration services could afford to live there. That's why all the young ones joined the academies, like Micah, Jade's mother, had done. Five years ago the fish stocks had started to decline and now the situation was desperate. The townsfolk were at their wits end and called a meeting to discuss what action they could take.

To Micah's surprise, Jade wanted to go to the meeting with her. They sat at the back and were listening intently to the discussion when suddenly Jade stood up and walked on to the stage. She stepped out in front of the whole townspeople and started to talk.

'Four years ago my father, Jacob, told you about the big pike in the lake and how it was taking the fish we eat. He pleaded for your help to kill it and when you refused, he attempted to do it himself. He died that night on the lake. Old Jack took him under the water and he was never seen again.' Jade paused for a moment as the memories came over her again like an emotional wave. 'Since then I have been studying the great galactic k-base and learned much about giant pike. Old Jack has become a master pike with a pack of young pike at his command. They bring him fish and he demands more and more to satisfy his massive hunger.'

The hall erupted with laughter. Old Jack is just a fairy tale they shouted in reply. We need serious suggestions and answers or we will all starve.

'I have the answer,' shouted Jade over the din. 'Old Jack has become fat and bloated. Tomorrow night the sky will be clear and the Tarset Moon will light up the lake. It will be our best chance to find and kill Old Jack. It will break the pack and balance will be restored to the lake.'

Jade was shouted down and she ran out of the hall in anger. Her mother followed her out very surprised by Jade's speech and how brave she had been. The next evening Jade prepared her gear and sneaked out of her bedroom window as quietly as possible, knowing her mother wouldn't approve.

For the last month she had been making a special lure that she'd learned about on the galactic knowledge base. It was half a meter long, made up of shiny tin can pieces all connected together with wire and a couple of viciously sharp hooks. In the water it would move like a large shiny fish and she was sure it would tempt Old Jack out of his hole.

Jade carefully tied the thin translucent carbon fibre line to the lure and the other end to a tree near the bank. She had a good idea where Old Jack would be, she had studied the terrain and found the likeliest spot. The Tarset Moon rose high and the water was clear. She slipped the lure into the water and using a long pole sent it out and moved it around in a figure of eight motion.

Two hours went by and just as Jade was beginning to get despondent, she saw a large shadow slowly tracking along the bank in the water. This was it, this was her chance to prove her father was right and get her revenge for his death. She swished the lure about a little faster and Old Jack pounced, snapping up the silvery fish like lure with the barbed hook sinking deep into his mouth. Old Jack thrashed around desperately trying to work the hook loose. Tying the line to the tree had been a good strategy, he was far too strong for Jade to catch just holding the pole.

After fifteen minutes it looked as though Old Jack was starting to tire but actually he was conserving his energy for a great leap. He could see Jade on the bank and he was going to pull her in and take out his rage on her. Just as Old Jack leapt out of the water towards the unsuspecting Jade, a huge spear went in through his left eye and out through his skull. Old Jack fell back into the water, dead. Micah had followed Jade and launched the spear from a few feet away.

She hugged Jade and told her how proud of her she was. They pulled Old Jack onto the bank and with a great effort tied all three and a half metres of him to Micah's speeder. They rode to town blasting the speeder's horn all the way. The townsfolk came out of their houses and cheered and danced when they saw the huge pike.

A great feast was made out of Old Jack the next day and Jade became the hero of the town. Over the next year the fish stocks in the lake improved just as she had predicted. The townsfolk were so grateful to Jade, they paid for her to study at the Tiri Academy for Natural Science and she became a renowned teacher.

MIKEY'S FIRST MISSION

Mikey was very excited about spending two whole weeks in the mountains with his mum and it'd felt like forever counting down the days. Not many seven year olds get to go on holiday in a space shuttle, let alone go to another planet.

Finlos was a small planet only a fifth of the size of Tiritane. Carol, Mikey's mum, was a band four shuttle pilot and she had been there many times. It had been a mining colony until the Berilamide became unviable. Huge amounts had been extracted for a hundred years but it was no longer cost effective.

The mining company, Ansos, had upheld its responsibilities and restored it back to a unique wilderness making it a beautiful wildlife sanctuary. Mikey was going to be a pilot just like his mum when he was older and he saw this trip as his first mission. The objective was to find a piece of Berilamide ore and bring it back to show it off to all his friends.

The sanctuary was huge and covered most of the planet.

They moved about to different regions every other day on the shuttle and it was a lot of fun. Mikey saw many birds and animals that he had only ever seen vis-clips of before.

With only three days left, Mikey still hadn't found his piece of ore even though he had been searching very hard. He was just about to give up hope of finding a piece when he glimpsed something shiny glinting in the sun, just down the little slope to his left in the remote valley they had found almost by accident.

As Mikey bent down to pick it up, the gritty gravel under his feet began to move then slide. Mikey was almost skiing on it now as he went slipping down a steep gully. Carol just saw the top of his head disappear as she came around the corner and called out for him to stay calm and not panic but she knew she couldn't follow him without getting caught up in the landslide too.

The gully opened up into a hole about a meter in diameter. Mikey fell through and slid even further down into a mine shaft. He landed with a bump up against a wall but he was ok and shouted back to his mum that he wasn't injured.

Carol went into automatic response mode like she was at work. She got on her communicator calling in the Rangers, giving precise coordinates sounding calm and professional but really she was starting to panic, just a little bit.

Mikey realised that actually he wasn't alright, he had a lump on his head and he was dizzy. Then everything started to fade and he passed out. The next thing he saw as he opened his eyes was a flickering light from a very bright head torch beam and it was dazzling him.

'There you are, I've been looking for you son. Come on let's get you up.'

A very large hand reached out and fully enclosed Mikey's small hand, pulling him up to his feet. He took a couple of wobbly steps and leaned against the man for support. Just then a large rock fell from the ceiling right where he had been sitting.

'Hey that was lucky,' said the man, 'we best make our way out to the gate before any more comes down.'

They set off along the tunnel and quickly came to a junction. It sloped up to the right and down to the left where there was some water lying.

'Down we go, keep left.' said the man confidently.

'Are you sure?' asked Mikey, he didn't like the look of the water.

'Oh yes, the water is shallow and round the next bend it slopes up to another junction, keep left again and you'll be at the gate. Don't worry son, I know these tunnels like the back of my hand.'

They set off at a steady pace, Mikey was feeling stronger now and, just as the man had said, they were at the next junction in no time.

'Ok son, off you go to the gate, they'll be waiting for you. I'm going back for the others.'

Before Mikey could say others, what others, he heard the gate clang and the sound of rusty hinges creaking. By the time he looked round again the man had gone, so Mikey ran up to the gate and emerged blinking into the light. Carol was there with a whole team of rangers and she grabbed Mikey for a big hug, just letting a tear slip down her cheek.

'Well, he's a clever young man for finding his way out all by himself. Well done.' said the chief ranger.

'No, the man you sent in found me and showed me the way.' said Mikey with a puzzled look on his face.

'But we've only just arrived, we were just about to get started, all my team are still here.'

Mikey suddenly realised he still had the shiny bit of metal

in his hand and when he looked closer he realised that it was a broken part of a name badge with the word 'Jack' engraved on it.

'No, surely not, it can't be!' exclaimed the ranger.

'Can't be what?' asked Carol.

'Well, there was a miner once, that everyone called Old Jack. He brought fifteen people out of this very gate after a tunnel collapsed. He went back in to find the two remaining miner's and was never seen again.'

'Do you think that was him then?' asked Mikey.

The ranger shook his head, 'I doubt it, that was twelve years ago.'

LB AND THE BLACK SHIP

Lynn and Bella were best friends, they went everywhere together. Their mums were best friends too, serving together as laser gun technicians on an ion hover ship. Joining the Sea Exploration Service Cadets at the age of twelve had been the best thing ever for Lynn and Bella. They excelled in earning all their competency badges and now at seventeen, they enrolled full time as protection guards for hover-ship cargo transporters.

They had full weapons and combat training. They were so good and worked so well together, it was like they had a psychic connection. They were always deployed together and simply known as LB in the SES. Some of the cargo was extremely valuable, especially the vehicle transporters.

There were occasional attacks on these missions from Skravian sea pirates. Old Jack and his black power-jet ship was the most notorious. He had a fierce reputation and most cargo ships gave up their goods without even a fight. When it appeared on the horizon, the Captain of the Navaro thought to himself, not this time Old Jack, we have LB.

Before the black ship was within pulse cannon range, LB had already deployed on their ion powered ski-jets. They hurtled forward at top speed, dodging laser pulses as they got nearer their target.

They drew alongside the ominous black ship, triggered the booster packs strapped to their backs and landed on the fore deck. They shot down the first four pirates easily and made their way into the ship. It was much more constrained in the dark passageways and fighting hand to hand they took out five more pirates. They cut their way through the corridors with machine-like efficiency. They captured a young pirate who gave up without a fight, the fear in his eyes was evident and LB interrogated him for the location of Old Jack.

'He's in the bridge and he's mad, he has us beaten by the Masterbot if we don't do as he says. The Masterbot is very dangerous, he has a laser whip and uses it often.'

LB carefully approached the bridge. As they turned the corner, a flash of laser whip snapped close to Bella's face. The whip from the Masterbot was flashing back and forth at great speed. Lynn set her blaster to rapid pulse and fired upwards from the bottom corner of the corridor spraying laser pulses off the walls in every direction. All the ricochet hit the Masterbot in its metal head and torso, rocking it backwards off balance. Bella launched herself forwards and thrust her laser dagger upwards through the jaw of the Masterbot right into its electronic brain.

Stepping over the smoking Masterbot, LB stood side by side on the bridge carefully looking around but there was no sign of Old Jack.

'Get off my ship scum before I have you skinned alive and fed to the sharks,' came a snarling menacing voice.

LB looked at each other and burst out laughing, Old Jack was literally in the bridge, it was the ship's Artificial Intelligence and it had become totally deranged.

Bella stabbed her laser dagger into the centre console with both hands and twisted it violently back and forth.

'Die Old Jack, you nasty old pirate. No more treasure for

you.'

Lynn could barely stop herself from falling over with laughter. The rest of the crew surrendered as soon as they knew the Masterbot was destroyed. LB transported them back to the Navaro on one of their own lifeboats, all tied up and ready for processing.

'Ready?' asked Lynn through her communicator.

'Go for it.' replied Bella.

Lynn hit the remote detonator to the plasma charges they had set and the big black ship exploded in a huge fireball before slowly sinking into the sea. LB giggled all the way back to the Navaro on their ski-jets.

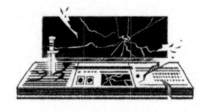

ALICE'S DREAM

Alice awoke with a start, it was the third night in a row she had had the same strange dream. It always started with her as a little girl, maybe three or four years old, sitting on her grandmother's lap. She couldn't have been any older as her grandmother had passed away just before her fifth birthday. They had been very close and spent a lot of time together. The dream ended with nine-year-old present day Alice waking in a panic and a cold sweat like she had been running or something but couldn't remember any more.

Alice's mother was a band one transport driver on the night shift, pulling hover containers from the sea port to the great city of Tiri. It was a tedious journey that went through the twenty kilometre long high-walled canyon of the Cygnas mountain range. Her father and older brother were deck cleaners, part of the maintenance gangs at the port. They weren't exactly poor but they occasionally struggled at times with rent credits. Overall though they were a happy family making the best of things.

Recent news reports were very worrying for the whole family. Three hover container drivers had gone missing in the great canyon. All along the canyon were fissures that opened up to sheer drops in the deep dark rocky valleys.

The band three ranger investigation hadn't found them or any signs of the hover containers. They had even sent a swarm of high tech camera drones but nothing had been found, it was a total mystery. The container runs had been suspended by the ranger command for two weeks but the port company put pressure on for them to resume due to the loss of revenue.

Alice's mum Lillian was keen to go back to work as well as they couldn't afford to lose any more credits. Rosa, their elderly next door neighbour who had been close friends with Alice's grandmother, said that it had happened before when she was young. A number of shepherds had gone missing while driving their rugged mountain sheep through the canyon and, in her opinion, Old Jack the rock troll had woken up and had eaten them.

'Old Jack, ha-ha, that's just a fairy tale mum used to tell me when I was a child,' laughed Lillian. 'Apparently mum and a bunch of her friends went to the middle of the canyon one night and put him to sleep with her little wooden flute, then a massive rock slide buried him forever.'

Alice remembered the wooden flute that her grandmother had played to her from when she was a baby. It had been the inspiration for her learning the flute too. Her seventh birthday had been the best day of her life when she received the silver plated one her parents had saved for years to buy her. She loved it, it was her most treasured possession. Rosa had given her lessons and she was very proud to be first flute in the school orchestra.

Lillian left for her first shift back to work. Alice had a really bad feeling and didn't want her to go but her mum wouldn't listen, she was confident everything would be okay. Alice struggled to get to sleep and finally dozed off about eleven o'clock. It was a fitful restless sleep and the dream started almost straight away.

'Alice, wake up, it's time to go,' it was her grandmother's voice, 'come on poppet, we don't have much time.'

Alice could see her in the distance, holding out her hand. She was younger than Alice remembered her, although detail was hard to make out. She caught up with her and took her hand, it was soft and warm, she had a firm grip but not too tight. Nana-b as she called her, the b was for Betty, had her little wooden flute in her other hand. Then Alice realised she was carrying her flute too. It all felt very real even though it was obviously a dream.

They were running along the road and soon came to the entrance of the canyon. There they joined some more shadowy figures, maybe five or six adults all holding hands with other children. To start with Alice didn't recognise anyone but then she saw Susan and Eric from school. Susan had her clarinet and Eric was holding his violin. They barely had time to wave to each other before they were off again at a pace.'

Time was being weird and all of a sudden they were at the centre of the canyon. A large fissure opened up on both sides like a crossroad and there was a sound of rumbling rocks coming from the left. Alice looked down the road and could just make out a couple of tiny pinpricks of light off in the far distance, a hover lorry was approaching from the city side.

'He's coming!' shouted Nana-b 'everyone line up in a semicircle around the opening to the left, hurry now, we must be quick.'

They gathered around and Susan and her grandfather started to play a slow melancholic tune on their clarinets. Eric and his grandmother joined in with their violins, quietly weaving in and around the melody. Suddenly there came a loud crunch of rock and then another like huge footsteps. It made all the children jump and interrupted the music.

'Don't stop, you must keep playing.' cried Nana-b.

The music resumed and began to get louder and quicker with others joining in. Alice could see Old Jack emerging from the fissure, he was huge, at least ten metres tall. His great rocky fists pulling at the edges of the fissure lifting himself up and out, with his long legs taking big strides onto the roadway. Her heart was racing and she was petrified. Her knees were trembling and she just wanted to turn and run away.

Nana-b started to play her wooden flute, she was looking right at Alice and Alice knew the tune straight away. It wasn't the same as the music already playing, it was like intertwining elements that eventually became the principal piece. Old Jack was stood in the middle of the little orchestral semicircle now. His huge granite head had two large red menacing eyes that glared at them and a massive jaw snapping open and shut rhythmically to the music. With clenched fists held out for balance, he lifted his right foot ready to stamp and crush them into the road.

Alice put her flute up to her mouth and began to play high and piercing notes. Old Jack started bring his foot downwards right towards Alice, but Nana-b played another set of notes almost like a duel to Alice's. Old Jack's foot slowed to a stop and then he began to rock backwards and forwards. When Alice played her part again, he stumbled back and fell over the edge of the fissure. Nana-b played the final notes of the piece, sharp and so loud that large cracks appeared at the edges of the fissure. One extra note from Alice brought the giant slabs crashing down on top of Old Jack burying him under thousands of tons of rock.

Alice woke up in a real panic, she was shaking uncontrollably and shouting incoherently. She opened her eyes and the morning light from the window was bright. There was a shadow right in front of her though and the thought of Old Jack's red eyes came into her mind but as she began to focus it softly faded to her mother's face.

She was holding Alice's hands and soothing her, calming her down. Alice hugged her mother tightly.

'Oh mum, I was so worried about you.'

'I'm fine poppet, the journey through the canyon was nothing to worry about. Although, on the way back there had obviously been a big rock slide. But no sign of that silly Old Jack.' she said with a big grin.

Alice couldn't wait to get to school and talk to Susan and Eric.

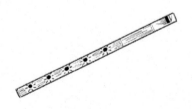

DAVEY'S BREAKDOWN

Davey was so upset and angry, he ran out of the hospital and all the way home. His dad Mark was very ill and only had a few weeks to live. It just wasn't fair and he was really struggling to deal with it. His other dad James was spending all the time he could at the hospital, but he was the only earner and worked long hours as well to keep the credits coming in.

Mark's work based medical insurance had covered his treatment plan so far and it had undoubtedly given him some extra months but now things had taken a turn for the worst and it was just a matter of time.

Davey was a bit of a loner. He didn't have many friends but the one best friend he did have was Hazel. Hazel was his next door neighbour and she was two years older than him. She had left last month on her fifteenth birthday to join the Ranger Academy.

He missed her so much, she had been like a big sister

always looking out for him, always ready to listen when he had problems or got bullied at school. But most of all she gave the best hugs. One hug from Hazel made everything better as far as he was concerned.

Davey had momentarily thought about contacting his birth mother Diane. She had been a surrogate for Mark and James and was a band three ranger pilot in the Tiritane Space Exploration Service. Davey hardly knew her though, she had occasionally turned up around his birthday for a couple of hours but she had no real duty or responsibility as a parent. She was currently off world on a two year mission so it wasn't practical anyway.

Right, said Davey to himself, I'm going to the city to find Hazel. And with that thought he got on his hover speeder and took off down the lane as fast as he could.

It was a junior speeder and a bit old, he'd had it for many years and had more or less out grown it. Tiri the great city was at least five hours away but Davey was determined to see Hazel. She was the only person in the world who would understand how he was feeling.

There was a big desert between Marsden, Davey's home town, and Tiri. There were rocky outcrops here and there but the road was a dusty track and there wasn't much traffic, especially in the evenings. Davey had taken a canister of water and a few snacks in his side bag but he hadn't thought about much else. He didn't even know the location of the Academy but he was sure he would be able to find it.

About two hours into the journey an amber light started to

flash on the central panel of his speeder. It had never done that before and Davey had no idea what it meant. If the speeder broke down he would be all alone in the desert and it was just starting to get dark. He started to think about the tales his dads used to tell him, about Old Jack the draxel.

Draxels were strange creatures, about the same size as a cheetah or puma but with a heavy bulbous tail. They didn't have any fur, just thick leathery skin with sharp claws and strong jaws with jagged teeth. They spent the hot days in burrows in the sand and emerged at night time when it was cooler. They generally ate small rodents and insects but had been known to take lone travellers who were unprepared.

Draxels could run very fast, often on two legs using their tail as a counter balance so the claws on their front legs could bring down their prey. Old Jack was a particularly large and nasty draxel that had eaten a number of children. Just tales said Davey to himself looking at the warning light again, just tales…

Half an hour later the amber light turned red and the hover engine spluttered for a few seconds and lost all power. Davey was stranded, he had no idea how to fix the speeder if indeed it could be. He was a bit less than halfway and wasn't sure whether to go on or go back.

After a few minutes of thinking it over, he thought he had best make his way home and try the journey another day. He pushed the speeder for a little while but it was too heavy so he left it on the side of the track.

He was trudging along feeling even sorrier for himself when he heard it - the strange gargling sound followed by hissing noises. It was dark now but there was just enough starlight to see the track and objects in the distance like the rocky boulders to his left.

The noises got louder and Davey could see a faint outline of an animal about a hundred metres to his right. It has to be Old Jack thought Davey, just starting to panic. He wasn't sure what to do and decided to make a run for the rocky outcrop. If he could climb up out of reach he would be safe until the morning.

Running as fast as he could, Davey soon realised that the rocks were much further away than he first thought and they were also much bigger. He could hear Old Jack behind him getting closer all the time. The gargling and hissing noises getting louder and faster, making him panic. He finally got to the boulders but they were huge and sheer faced and he couldn't find any grips or foot hold to climb up.

Davey turned around with his back to the rocks and saw the draxel coming all wild eyes and lolling tongue with large claws reaching out towards him. Then a blinding light appeared and Davey put his arm up to shield his eyes, expecting the beast to tear into him any second. He could feel the spittle from its slobbering mouth and a claw scraped at his jacket but it seemed to be held back somehow. Then there was a dull thud and a cracking noise followed by gurgling.

Davey lowered his arm and blinking in the brightness he saw the blade of a hunting knife protruding from the throat of the draxel. It slumped to the ground to reveal an old lady standing on its tail behind it. The lights were from a hover hire transporter that had Davey's speeder coupled up to the rear bumper. The woman was about seventy five years old, had long reddish-grey hair and was slim but strong looking.

'Well young man, what are you doing out here by yourself? You know, you should have special filters for the sand fitted to your speeder if you are travelling in the desert.'

'I – I was – I' he stammered.

Davey couldn't speak, his shoulders started shaking and a wave of tears just burst out of him. He had been very stupid and hadn't thought anything through properly. He slumped down and sat against the rock. Then it all came tumbling out, the whole story about his dad and how upset he'd been and wanting to see his friend. It had all got too much for him and he wasn't coping at all.

The woman sat down beside him, held his hand and listened intently. She said 'oh', 'ah' and 'I see' at just the right moments then gave him a huge hug that was almost as good as one from Hazel.

'Come on then Davey, let's get you home.'

She walked him to her vehicle, it had 'Jacqueline's Transport Hire' written on the side.

'Thank you Jacqueline, for saving me from the draxel.'

'Oh, you're very welcome Davey, but no one has called me Jacqueline for years. The folk in town call me Old Jack the taxi but my friends just call me Jack' she replied with a smile. 'It's lucky that I was on my way back from a fare in the city. I tell you what though, the next time I go, I'll take you to see Hazel.'

Davey gave Jack another big hug. He was so happy to have a new friend.

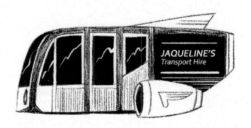

ELLY AND STEPHEN

Elly and Stephen were on the last day of their honeymoon when the call came in. The ten days they had spent together after their partner for life ceremony had been wonderful. The wildlife sanctuary on Finlos covered two thirds of the small planet and had been re-wilded after the Berilamide ore had started to run out. The rest of the planet still had some small mining outposts here and there but they weren't very profitable any more.

Being talented artists, Elly and Stephen loved their jobs illustrating, photographing and producing wildlife marketing materials for the Tiritane Space Exploration Service. They were also band two reserve explorers and could be called on at any time to help or investigate in an emergency.

Reports of a monster terrorising a small community in the northern most region of the planet had come over the ranger network. It was outside of the sanctuary but as they were the nearest explorers they were duty bound to investigate. The fact that they were experts in animals and wildlife would also be a good advantage in determining what kind of threat it was.

The reports were vague - some kind of large beast had taken a child. When the villagers tracked it down, three of them had been killed and two more had been badly injured. The winters in the North had been particularly harsh recently and food sources were scarce. The villagers hunted wild animals to supplement their winter stores but this year it seemed they were the ones being hunted.

Stephen went through the weapons inventory and updated himself on the protocols from the service regulations. They passed their weapons certification every year as required but they had never been in a situation quite like this before. Elly and Stephen didn't really like weapons and had avoided conflict as much as possible in their career. It was an essential part of their role but wildlife and artwork had been the real reason for joining the service in the first place.

Elly powered up the shuttle and gave the coordinates to Dave, the shuttle's Artificial Intelligence.

'Expected arrival in three hours and fifteen minutes Elly,' came the reply from Dave.

'What's the weather report like for the area Dave?' asked Stephen.

'Minus ten Celsius, light easterly winds, ten centimetres of lying snow but no more snowfall expected in the next few days Stephen.'

Elly pushed on the thrusters and they were off. The remote

village was in a forest that had a river running through it. The Berilamide there had been too difficult to extract but there was just enough silver ore to attract a few hardy families, and over time the small community had grown to about a hundred people. Setting the shuttle down in a clearing on the outskirts of Cerak, Elly and Stephen put on their thermal suits and went to meet with Kelvin, the village marshal.

'After many years of absence, Old Jack the great white wolf has returned to the area. He has grown very large and has a voracious appetite. He has killed four including young Billy who was only six years old.' said Kelvin looking very concerned. 'We tracked him to the caves in the forest near the river and shot at him with pulse laser rifles but they seemed to have no effect. The laser pulses just scatter like he has some sort of force shield or armour.'

Elly looked at Stephen, it was worse than they had feared and all hopes of capturing the beast were quickly disappearing. Both of them hated the thought of killing an animal but there didn't seem to be a choice, it was going to be them or Old Jack.

'I remember reading about a type of hare that had hollow strands of fur. In the winter the strands turned translucent and reflected the snow as a camouflage.' said Elly. 'At a certain temperature though, the fur took on a crystalline coating making it refract lasers. The weapons division got very excited about it, hoping to develop a new type of shield. Maybe it's the same with Old Jack'

'Well if that's the case,' said Stephen, 'laser pulse weapons will indeed be useless. I don't suppose you have any old fashioned firearms and ammunition here Kelvin?'

'No, the only other weapons we have are spears and knives.'

'Maybe we should wait for backup then.' said Stephen.

'Dave reckons five days until we get any help, which is too long. Let's get it done as soon as possible eh? These poor people need help and they need it now.' said Elly with a determined look on her face.

Kelvin provided Elly and Stephen with spears, they already had their own knives.

'Well,' said Elly 'I'm still going to bring my laser pulse rifle, maybe his legs or head may not be protected by his winter coat.'

After they checked their packs, ropes and other kit, they set off towards the caves. Walking through the village was eerily quiet with no sign of anyone. All the houses were locked up, no lights or fires, everyone was hiding away. It was obvious that the villagers were terrified of Old Jack.

The path through the forest was easy to follow and they were near the caves in about an hour. Kelvin pointed out where the last battle had taken place, describing the action in detail.

'We need to draw him out into an open space, fighting here in these cave entrances would give him the advantage.' said Stephen looking around.

'The river has frozen over. It's the only open space nearby but the ice is thick enough to walk on safely.' said Kelvin pointing to the gap in some bushes that lead to the river.

Just as they were quietly discussing this, Stephen caught a slight movement to his right. He could just make out a faint outline of something definitely four legged and very large, maybe five feet tall at the shoulder.'

He gave a small hand signal to the others and the three of them slowly moved further apart. Stephen began to turn cautiously to his right gripping the shaft of his spear tight. Then they heard it, a snarling menacing growling and a split second later a massive jaw with sharp teeth ripped through Stephen's suit near his shoulder.

He spun around as fast as he could thrusting the spear at the neck of the beast but he wasn't quick enough and the jaw clamped onto the spear shaft ripping it from his grasp. Elly and Kelvin both ran forward stabbing their spears as hard as they could into the body of Old Jack but they just seemed to glance off.

Stephen started to run towards the ice bound river but Old Jack followed, snapping his teeth into Stephen's backpack and dragging him from side to side in a wrenching movement. Struggling as he was, Stephen managed to pull a small bottle from his pocket and squirted a liquid over his shoulder into Old Jack's eyes. Then, slashing his knife across the straps of his backpack, Stephen ran further out onto the middle of the ice. Old Jack was blinded but his very keen senses of smell and hearing could still triangulate Stephen's trajectory and followed after him in a massive rage, howling with pain from his burning eyes.

Meanwhile, Elly had unshouldered her laser pulse rifle and tied it to the rope she had ready. She threw it as hard as possible across the ice towards Stephen. He dived onto it and rolled a few times wrapping the rope around his body. Old Jack was nearly on him and launched up to pounce down on his prey. Stephen fired the pulse laser, but not at Old Jack, instead he fired down and at the ice all around himself.

The ice started to hiss and crack, Old Jack could hear it but he was already committed to his leap. He crashed down right on top of Stephen and they both went through into the freezing water. Elly and Kelvin pulled hard as they could on the rope and Stephen came back to the surface. The current of the river pulled Old Jack further under the ice and he became trapped. After a few minutes of clawing desperately at the underside of the ice, the great white wolf drowned.

Dragging Stephen out and back to the bank, Kelvin pulled some blankets from his pack and started to wrap them around him. Stephen was barely conscious and just about breathing. Elly was trying to warm him up as quickly as possible, rubbing his hands and cracking the ice off his bearded face.

'Wow,' said Kelvin, 'what did he spray in Old Jack's face? I've never seen anything like that before.'

Stephen opened one eye, lifted a finger in a wagging motion and said 'never - ever - go out, without some chilli sauce!'

JULIE'S FATE

Julie looked out of the dormitory window again. It was her first night at the academy summer training camp, the sun was going down and the sky was turning a deep red. She had been a cadet for a year now and when she turned fourteen last month, her mother finally agreed to let her do the Explorer Orienteering Course.

Julie's mother and older sister had been there when they were young and often told stories about how hard the training was. There would be lots of fitness marches, map reading lessons and obstacle courses. Plenty of swimming and running would culminate in a twenty kilometre race on the last day.

Julie wasn't fazed by any of this, she was always training. She loved physical workouts and she could already read maps and the directional phase emitters connected to vehicles. What she was really intrigued by was the stories about the fate tree. An ancient tree that had been struck by lightning many years ago. It was very large and had a hollow in the trunk that you could walk into.

If you stood in the hollow at midnight you would supposedly learn your fate and see your future career. Apparently, only strong willed courageous people saw their true future. Lazy or timid cadets saw a terrible death and were chased out of the tree by a monster called Old Jack.

Julie's mother would never speak about her experience and made her daughters promise to avoid the tree entirely. Sharon,

Julie's elder sister told her that she went in and nothing happened at all but she never let on to her mum that she had disobeyed her.

For three nights in a row, Julie tried not to think about it but the next evening she couldn't sleep and she felt compelled to go out and investigate. She crept out of the dorm and walked the half kilometre to the fate tree at the edge of the forest. It was a cloudy night, warm but quite windy and the branches of the tree were swaying and creaking loudly.

Julie stepped into the hollow. It was very dark and it took a few moments for her eyes to adjust. Just then she heard a sobbing that sounded as though it came from below. When she looked down she could see a faint light coming through the cracks in a trap door. She found the iron loop and pulled the door up and open. Below was a wooden ladder going down to a narrow but tall, stone lined tunnel.

There was a series of dim emergency lights spaced about two metres apart giving enough light for Julie to see a boy lying on the floor holding his ankle. She carefully climbed down the rickety wooden ladder but as she reached the bottom, the trap door suddenly slammed shut and the ladder collapsed into a pile of broken pieces. Julie and the injured boy were trapped.

The slim looking boy didn't appear to be much older than twelve and Julie could just make out the name Kam on his jacket badge.

'Hey Kam, are you ok? Is your ankle badly injured? Can you walk at all?'

Kam stopped sobbing and looked up at Julie. 'I think it's broken, it hurts so much I don't think I can stand let alone walk.'

'Well this tunnel must come out somewhere but which way is best?'

The decision was made for them in the next few seconds, a horrible screeching and howling sound came from up the tunnel to the left.

'It's Old Jack!' exclaimed Kam with a look of sheer terror on his face, 'we have to get out of here now!'

He tried to get up and Julie helped him to stand but his ankle gave way again and he fell back down with a scream of pain. The terrifying noises were getting louder and they were sure they could also hear a scrabbling, scratching sound like claws on stones.

Julie managed to get Kam standing again and propped him up against the tunnel wall before turning around and pulling his arms around her neck to give him a piggy back. With one hand she just managed to grab a longish wooden rail from the ladder pile and set off running as fast as she could.

The sounds of the beast grew louder and louder and it felt as though Old Jack was only a few metres behind them. Kam was in terrible pain and the tunnel seemed to go on and on before them.

'We're not going to make it, he's going to get us. I wish I'd never come here.' said Kam.

'No, don't lose hope Kam, we're going to get out of here, I just know it.'

A moment later they saw a door off in the distance. When

they reached it Julie grabbed at the handle but it was locked. She carefully put Kam down and tried again to no avail. Looking back down the tunnel they could make out movement in the shadows. The screeching howling and scraping rang in their ears and they were both absolutely terrified.

Julie took a very deep breath. She raised the wooden stick above her head and charged towards the monster letting out the loudest scream she could. She ran for maybe thirty metres but there was no sign or sound of it - the monster had disappeared. She caught her breath and turned to see the door opening. A man was helping Kam up and out. By the time Julie got there a woman in a smart uniform was waiting for her, holding the door open.

'Well done cadet, you have shown exemplary conduct helping your comrade and showing real courage in the face of danger.'

Julie breathed a sigh of relief as they walked through the door and out into the warm night air. She turned to talk to the woman but she wasn't there anymore. The tunnel door had disappeared too and she found herself standing in front of the fate tree. She was shocked and surprised then an image of the rangers name badge came into her mind. It said 'Julie Ranger Pilot' and had five bars engraved on it to show band five of the service, the highest level you could achieve.

RAE AND THE STONE

Rae rolled her eyes. 'Fine,' she said grumpily, 'you can come along if you want to but it's not your challenge.'

'I know, I know,' said Andrew 'but there is nothing in the rules to say you have to go alone. It's a long way and that old castle will be very dangerous at this time of year with ice and frost on those old stones.'

'I'm not scared you know, I've done bigger challenges than this before.'

'Yes, but what if you slip and bang your head on the slippery stones? I won't interfere with the challenge, I just want to make sure you get back safe. That's all.'

It was New Year's Day. Rae and Andrew had been at the New Year's Eve party the night before with their friends from Tiritane University. They had met up every year since graduation and it was a tradition to gather at the Hikers Knee Inn for the challenge. On the stroke of midnight they had each taken an envelope from the old rucksack and read out their challenge. Andrew picked the only reoccurring one that everybody had done before. He was to take their club mascot, a roughly carved wooden mountain goat the size of a small dog called 'Bounce', to the top of the Kerin Peak the next day by three pm and take a selfie for proof.

Three years ago when Andrew had first done the challenge, he had beaten Rae's record from the year before by twenty minutes. The bickering arguments about which path was taken or the weather conditions had resulted in them initially falling out. Then a joint race the following week to finally settle the issue ended in a draw. That's when they fell in love and they'd been together ever since.

Rae's challenge this year was to hike the thirty kilometres over the hilly moorlands to Anbar Castle on the coast. Just getting there would be challenge enough but it had to be timed just right. She was to arrive on the evening of the first full moon of the year on the 28th of January. The castle is a privately owned ruin that was closed for the winter. She was to get into the middle of the courtyard and take a selfie with her head on the old stone.

'Is that it?' said Rae at the time, 'easy peasy.'

'Oh, I don't know,' said Tommy, 'watch out for Old Jack the executioner! He's got a really sharp sword, he used to cut heads off on that old stone.'

'Yeah right, maybe he did but that was hundreds of years ago.' said Rae with a laugh.

The morning was drifting by. Andrew left to do his

challenge and Rae started planning hers. It would be a ten hour hike over the moors but with only eight hours of daylight at this time of year she would need to set off before dawn. At least the first hour would be on the firm wide bridleway, that would help, and the last hour would be along the grassy fields sloping up to the castle.

Anbar Castle was perched on a rocky outcrop overlooking the coast. The east wall of the great hall was on the cliff edge with a high pointed gable overlooking the twenty five metre drop to the beach below.

The southern end of the castle wall was in the poorest condition with the round tower in the corner mostly in ruin. That would be her way in to get to the courtyard in the middle. The great hall had a large round window with deep red stained glass to catch the sunrise. The rest of the hall had been destroyed by fire long ago.

The weeks and days passed by slowly but the challenge finally began. The weather was frosty but there was very little wind and the forecast was for a clear day with temperatures of about one or two Celsius. They set off at six am and went at a fair pace. After about an hour and a half they stopped for a quick snack. That was when Andrew realised that Rae had sneaked Bounce the goat into his rucksack.

'I thought it felt heavier than it should, that's not very nice of you adding extra weight like that.'

'Well Andrew, if you're coming with me it should at least be a bit of a challenge for you too.' said Rae with a cheeky grin.

Being experienced hikers they covered the distance easily and without any drama. They had another brief stop for lunch and it was dark by the time they approached the castle. The last wispy clouds of the day drifted out to sea and the stars shone brightly.

Scrambling up the ruined southern tower, they emerged onto the top of wall as the moon rose. Andrew sat on the wall with the rucksacks and Rae went down the slippery steps into the courtyard. The moon aligned with the great hall window that sent a strange and eerie reddish light, which put a pinkish glow about the stone.

Rae leaned over the stone and saw the stars reflected in the trough of water next to it that had yet to re-freeze. She was rummaging in her pocket for her camera when a shadow passed over the reflection. A sudden panic came over her and she just managed to push herself away when a great sword that had a large ruby set into the pommel of the handle, rang off the stone with a loud clang.

The noise was still vibrating in her ears as she turned to see Old Jack the executioner, looming over her getting ready for another swing. He was made of shadow, pure blackness, and as solid as the stone itself edged with a thin ruby coloured line. He was at least two metres tall with broad shoulders and big muscular arms.

Rae took a step back as the sword slashed in front of her cutting through the layers of her fleece lined coat and thermal jumper and ripping a five centimetre line along her waist about a millimetre or so deep. Rae could feel the blood oozing out of the cut, it wasn't much more than a scratch but it had scared the life out of her. She pulled her coat tight as she ran for the steps of the tower.

Andrew had heard the clang of the sword and the screaming and swearing Rae let out when the sword bit her. He could see Old Jack striding after her across the courtyard. The moonlight was pouring in through the big round window and it was almost like Old Jack was a hologram being projected by the eerie red light that focused like a beam on the ruby in his sword.

Rae was at the tower steps but Old Jack was almost on her, lifting the great sword above his head for the final strike. Andrew grabbed Bounce from his rucksack and ran along the wall a few metres. It was just enough distance to give him the angle he needed and he launched the wooden goat at the window. Rae lost her footing on the third step and fell backwards. Looking up to see the sword coming down towards her she closed her eyes and waited for it to cut through.

The roughly carved wooden goat crashed right through the window at exactly the same time and the spell was broken. Rae opened one eye to see Old Jack dissipating into the night sky. Andrew ran down the steps and scooped her up, hugging her tightly.

'Wow, I thought I had lost you,' he said as the tears welled up in both their eyes.

'Nope!' said Rae defiantly, 'but you've lost Bounce and if you don't find him before we go back in the morning you'll get thrown out of the club.'

ABOUT THE AUTHOR

Roy Pendle is from the Midlands of England. Born in the 1960s, he grew up with children's science fiction television programmes that led him into sci-fi and fantasy fiction from many authors. Roy used to tell his young children about an entity called Old Jack that he made up while on family holidays. They're grown up now and he spends his time restoring bits of old furniture, roaming about the beautiful Northumberland coastline, and writing stories.

For more information about Roy and read the bonus Old Jack tale - Janey's Story. Visit: www.pendle.me.uk

Janey's House

Printed in Great Britain
by Amazon